MW00934218

FOREVERMORE

VMH™ Publishing
Atlanta, GA

VMH™ Publishing
3355 Lenox Rd. NE Ste 750
Atlanta, GA 30326
vmhpublishing.com

The publisher is not responsible for websites, or social media pages (or their content) related to this publication, that are not owned by the publisher. Quantity sales. Special discounts are available on quantity purchases by corporations, associations, and others. For details, contact the publisher via email at: info@vmhpublishing.com

Hardback ISBN: 978-1-947928-77-0

Published in United States of America

10 9 8 7 6 5 4 3 2 1

Dedication

This book is dedicated to my love ones, especially my grandchildren, Parker, Vin, Alexandra and James. They are my inspiration for writing this book. Also to my God, who loves all His children.

FOREVERMORE

Written by: Bobbye McNish

Illustrations by: Feenix Fabay

Bithia quickly ran upstairs to her room. She threw herself upon the bed, buried her face in her hands, and started to cry. She was tired of feeling angry and sad all the time. She wanted to see her friends, go to school and feel happy. Thoughts and emotions raced through her head and heart. She wondered, if there was a way for hope and joy to return to her heart, instead of the loneliness and sadness she felt inside?

Her crying was interrupted by a sudden strong wind that rushed across her body. Sounds of fluttering wings roared in her ears. A huge white bird with a face of a dove landed upon her pillow. "Come with me and learn the answer to your question,"

said the bird. Bithia was afraid, but the bird's eyes and voice were gentle and calming, so she climbed upon its back. Off they flew through the walls of her bedroom and into the sky to find the answer.

The bird brought Bithia to a majestic crystal temple with a river, as clear as glass, which flowed down in front of it. The leaves on the trees looked like green glass. She noticed how the water and trees sparkled in the light of day. As Bithia was admiring a huge tree on the side of the river, the bird told her it was called the Tree of Life. The tree had twelve different types of fruit on it for each month of the year. While she stood there, she heard lovely sounds of musical instruments and voices singing. She wished earth was this beautiful and peaceful.

Bithia followed the sounds into the crystal temple. Inside, a man dressed all in white and wearing a golden sash sat upon a throne with a rainbow all around it. His hair was white as wool. His eyes sparkled like flames of fire and his face glowed like the morning sun. Bithia gazed at the four living creatures around his throne. They were strange creatures whose shapes were like a lion, an ox, an eagle, and one Bithia could not describe. Each one had six wings and eyes that could see all around them. They repeated, "holy, holy, holy" to the man.

Bithia started to walk toward the man, but was blocked by two giant angels dressed in armor carrying flaming swords. The man quickly stood up from his throne and in a firm voice declared, "Do not stop the

children from coming to me. I have a plan and purpose for them." Then in a gentle voice, he welcomed Bithia to the Kingdom of Forevermore and told her his name, Lord Sabaoth. Sabaoth means the Lord of Hosts or angel army. He said many call him by other names, such as, Jesus, Savior, Prince of Peace and King of Kings. Bithia noticed rows of shelves like in a library. There were so many books that she could not see the end of the shelves. She asked the man, "Why are there so many books?" He explained that everyone on earth has their own book in Forevermore. The books contain the wonderful plans created for a person's life. This is why, he had brought Bithia to his kingdom. Bithia's book was brought forward, and he read her name which meant, daughter of God. He read

about the plan for her to tell other children about Forevermore and how to join with Lord Sabaoth to overcome the attacks of their hearts.

Lord Sabaoth told Bithia about a Red Dragon with ten horns and a long tail. The Red Dragon had once been good, but had tricked people with his words to disobey the rules of Lord Sabaoth. After their disobedience, the people's hearts were open for attacks. Since the Red Dragon had disobeyed, Lord Sabaoth ordered him to leave Forevermore. The Red Dragon was now hiding on earth, so he would not be noticed.

Bithia fell to her knees and started to cry as she thought about the Red Dragon hiding on earth. She was a little girl and he was a big Red Dragon. Lord Sabaoth reached for Bithia's right hand and lifting her up, said, "I will help you! I am the commander of a large angel army. I will teach you how the Red Dragon attacks your heart and how to overcome his schemes. Do not be afraid, for I will always be with you." Then a rushing mighty wind came upon her. She could feel a change in her heart. Lord Sabaoth stated, "Now, my spirit will always be within your heart."

What felt like hours was only seconds as Lord Sabaoth instructed Bithia in what she was to tell the other children. He had given the book called the Bible to the adults, but many no longer read or obeyed it. The Bible was a powerful weapon to overcome the schemes of the Red Dragon. Sadly, many

adults no longer believed Lord Sabaoth existed or would come back for them. He was not late in keeping his promise to return, but in the Kingdom of Forevermore, time is not the same. One day is like a thousand years and a thousand years is like one day. His delay is from his love in wanting more people to come live in the Kingdom of Forevermore. For now, they were to use the weapons he had given them to overcome the Red Dragon. Lord Sabaoth said the time was soon coming for him and his angel army to capture and chain the Red Dragon into a bottomless pit.

"Bithia, will you go back and tell the children to believe in Lord Sabaoth and to use the weapons I have given them? I want the children to know, they can have hope

and a good future ahead of them. If they follow my ways, I will heal and change their hearts." A part of her was not sure she could do it, but something inside of her rose up and with a shout of excitement, she said, "Yes, I will tell them!" "Go now Bithia and watch out for the Red Dragon. He is always looking to steal the goodness and joy from the heart. Remember, I will hear you, when you call out to me." With a nod of his head as to say, "goodbye" and with a smile on his face, Lord Sabaoth vanished from her sight.

She found herself, once again upon the back of the huge white bird with a dove's face headed for home. They had almost arrived, when Bithia heard, "Are you looking for me?" She quickly turned her head to see the face of the Red Dragon with

his ten horns, then she saw his whole body. Wham! He bumped into the bird with such force that it sent Bithia flying backwards to the ground. As she started to stand up, she shouted, "It's all your fault! In a sly voice, the Red Dragon, asked Bithia to join him in ruling the earth. He would give her whatever she wanted. She could rule over others like he did. He crept closer to Bithia, and with a flick of his tail, red, orange and yellow fiery darts shot out towards her. The Red Dragon laughed an evil laugh, "Now, I will have your heart too."

Remembering Lord Sabaoth's words, Bithia yelled, "Lord Sabaoth, I need you!" As quickly as he had vanished, Lord Sabaoth was with her. He handed Bithia a Bible. It flew open into a giant shield with a

cross and twelve beautiful stones on it. Bithia read the words written on the back of the shield. She was stunned to see all the words in the Bible. Lord Sabaoth told her to read the words aloud and to believe in them. As she spoke the words, "No weapon that comes against me will win," and "Resist the Red Dragon and he will flee from you," the shield of faith protected her. She could see her words turning into flaming swords destroying the Red Dragon's fiery darts. Lord Sabaoth spoke the words, "Greater am I and my angel army, than you are Red Dragon in this world." His words became a double edge sword cutting the darts into tiny pieces. Bithia was amazed and happy to see how powerful the words of the Bible can be used to overcome the Red Dragon. Seeing he was losing, the Red Dragon quickly fled.

Lord Sabaoth reminded Bithia to always have her armor of the Bible and faith in its words to walk in victory.

Bithia jumped with joy. She had found her answer! With Lord Sabaoth and the words in the Bible, she had overcome the schemes of the Red Dragon. Now, she knew the way to defend herself from the fiery darts. No longer would her heart remain feeling sad and without hope.

"Bithia, I must go back to Forevermore and prepare for my return to capture and chain the Red Dragon. But remember, I am always watching over you and my spirit is within your heart. Tell the children what you learned. Tell them, they were born for such a time as this." He handed Bithia a white stone with a golden fish symbol. Everyone

who believes in me will receive a white stone to come celebrate with me in Forevermore.

Suddenly, Bithia found herself standing in front of her house. She ran inside and upon seeing Abel, her little brother, she told him about Lord Sabaoth, the Kingdom of Forevermore and how to overcome the Red Dragon. Every day since, Bithia told friends, children at school, or in her neighborhood what she learned. She wanted all the children to know the hope and love Lord Sabaoth brings to their hearts and never forget he is coming soon!

About The Author

Bobbye McNish is a teacher, writer, and lover of nature. It's through writing, she finds her way of expressing God's beautiful message of hope and His plans to younger children.

Bobbye has over 35 years of public school educational experience, taught Christian curriculum, and served youth with disabilities in the juvenile justice system. She has a master's degree in Special Education and Certification in Educational Leadership.

She lives in Marietta, GA with her husband, David, and dog named Maddie. She has two daughters and four grandchildren. May this book not only touch the hearts of the children, but also to the adults who read it.

Find out more about Bobbye at: www.Bobbyemcnish.com

CPSIA information can be obtained
at www.ICGtesting.com
Printed in the USA
BVHW020952100721
611456BV00023B/455